Dear Parent:
Your child's love of reading starts here!

Every child learns to read in a different way and at his or her own speed. Some go back and forth between reading levels and read favorite books again and again. Others read through each level in order. You can help your young reader improve and become more confident by encouraging his or her own interests and abilities. From books your child reads with you to the first books he or she reads alone, there are I Can Read Books for every stage of reading:

SHARED READING
Basic language, word repetition, and whimsical illustrations, ideal for sharing with your emergent reader

BEGINNING READING
Short sentences, familiar words, and simple concepts for children eager to read on their own

READING WITH HELP
Engaging stories, longer sentences, and language play for developing readers

READING ALONE
Complex plots, challenging vocabulary, and high-interest topics for the independent reader

ADVANCED READING
Short paragraphs, chapters, and exciting themes for the perfect bridge to chapter books

I Can Read Books have introduced children to the joy of reading since 1957. Featuring award-winning authors and illustrators and a fabulous cast of beloved characters, I Can Read Books set the standard for beginning readers.

A lifetime of discovery begins with the magical words "I Can Read!"

Visit www.icanread.com for information
on enriching your child's reading experience.

The Berenstain Bears Play Football! Copyright © 2017 by Berenstain Publishing, Inc. All rights reserved. Manufactured in China.
No part of this book may be used or reproduced in any manner whatsoever without written permission except in the case of brief
quotations embodied in critical articles and reviews. For information address HarperCollins Children's Books, a division of
HarperCollins Publishers, 195 Broadway, New York, NY 10007.
www.icanread.com

Library of Congress Control Number: 2016944511
ISBN 978-0-06-235034-3 (trade bdg.) — ISBN 978-0-06-235033-6 (pbk.)

17 18 19 20 21   SCP   10 9 8 7 6 5 4 3 2 1
❖
First Edition

The Berenstain Bears®
PLAY FOOTBALL!

Mike Berenstain

Based on the characters created by
Stan and Jan Berenstain

HARPER

An Imprint of HarperCollinsPublishers

It's time for football in Bear Country.

The Grizzly Bowl is on TV today.

The Bear family is having a Grizzly

Bowl party.

Family and friends gather at the
Bears' home.

There is a lot of food. There is a

lot to drink.

Everyone is talking and laughing.

Everyone is having a good time.

The TV is turned on for the game.

The cubs sit down to watch.

But there is just a lot of talking.

In between the talking,

there are a lot of ads.

"When does the game start?"

asks Brother.

"It doesn't start for hours yet," says Papa.

"They just talk about it first."

"Oh," says Brother.

The cubs are all bored.

They decide to go outside to play.

"What should we play?" asks Sister.

A football is lying on the grass.

"FOOTBALL!" everyone shouts.

The cubs choose teams.

They start to play.

Honey gets the ball.

She is small.

She runs between the other players' legs.

She scores a touchdown!

Now the other side has the ball.

They are all big.

They run right through the other players.

They score a touchdown, too.

Grizzly Gran is bored.

She is tired of all the talking on TV.

She is tired of getting food for everyone.

She looks out the window.

She sees the cubs playing football.

That looks like fun!

Gran goes outside.

"May I join you?" she asks the cubs.

"YAY!" the cubs shout. "Gran is
going to play!"
Gran joins the team of Brother,
Sister, and Honey.

"Now, here's my plan,"

whispers Gran.

Gran's team lines up.

"Thirty-three! Forty-four! Fifty-five!

HIKE!" yells Gran.

Brother hikes the ball to Gran.

Gran pretends to give the ball to Sister.

The other team follows Sister.

But Gran still has the ball.

She throws a long pass.

Brother catches it.

Touchdown!

Grizzly Gramps wants more food.

"Where's Gran?" he asks.

He sees her outside playing football.

"That looks like fun!" says Gramps.

He goes outside, too.

"Say," says Papa, "where's Gramps?"

He sees Gramps outside playing football.

"Hey, everybody!" he says.

"That looks like fun.

Let's all play!"

All the grown-ups go outside.

They start playing football.

They have a great time!

At last, the Grizzly Bowl comes on TV.

But there is no one to watch it.

Because they are all *playing* football.

Go team!